I Wed the Sea

I Wed the Sea

Lauren G. Flanagan

IGUANA

Publisher: Meghan Behse
Editor: Amanda Feenley
Cover art: David Morris (www.islandsunstudio.com)

ISBN 978-1-77180-476-9 (paperback)
ISBN 978-1-77180-477-6 (epub)

This is an original print edition of *I Wed the Sea*.

*This book is dedicated to my nephew, who
died too young.*

*J. Dylan White
1989–2015*

*This is how we must love it, faithful and
fleeting. I wed the sea.*

—Albert Camus, *The Sea Close By*

Prologue

The first time I ever saw him, I wasn't ready to really see him. So I didn't. I missed it.

There was a quietness about him, a stillness. He looked like he might radiate overconfidence, but he didn't. In time, I came to know that he is always like this—like a sunrise, at peace. He loves the sea because he feels at one with the sun, the sea, the sand. He doesn't *need* the ocean like I do. It's not his church.

We are all time travelers. Our planet hurtles through the universe, shedding lives, like stardust. In its wake, he is there. We all are. I wish I could run straight into the sunrise fast enough, on and on, and into yesterday, and yesterday, and yesterday, and keep going, through sunrise after sunrise, faster and faster, and find her, me. I would tell her…hurry.

Sunrise

I grew up in the sea and poverty was sumptuous, then I lost the sea and found all luxuries grey…
—Albert Camus, *The Sea Close By*

It's still dark.

She lifts the heron blue blanket from the weathered white bench. She removes the ivory wrap from its home on the hook. She whispers, "Come on Ben." As ebony fades to slate, they make their way to the beach. The light hints of secrets. The katydids cease buzzing. It is a cool misty morning. The sun is still shy.

Cresting the dunes, they arrive at that magic moment when the stars vanish, eclipsed by the sun. The rolling waves are a tender lullaby. The white foam is eerily bright. The air is full of the smell of the salt and the sand. The *sea*.

Gulls, sentimental sentinels, stare at the horizon. They are the wives of sailors who have been out to sea for far too long or are never coming home.

Silently, like a sorcerer turning silver into gold, the sun rises. It's not an exact moment, more like many moments strung together, like a lifetime. The first rays of light settle on her. She takes a deep breath. As she breathes out, she slowly releases the sand from her clenched hands. Sand slivers through her fingers. The sky is burnt orange blazing into white.

The sun rises and, as promised, I feel renewed. Sitting quietly beside me is Ben, my best friend, my soulmate, my dog. The sunrise feels like it's only for us. The seagulls let out their first of many cries, calling good morning to the day. I am slowly running my hands along Ben's fur when he stands and runs up the beach. I turn and see a man and his dog. Both of our dogs are Labradors, only Ben is a Chocolate and his is a Yellow. The dogs act like long-lost friends. It's almost as if they didn't know they were lonely until they met each other.

When your dogs decide that they are a *thing*, their people kind of have to meet. Plus, we are alone, on a beach, at sunrise.

The man approaches me and comments on the dogs, which are now bravely attempting a dip in the sea. It's spring and the water is as cold as chaos. The dogs think better of swimming and run up to the dunes. He introduces himself, and I tell him that I am Eve. We exchange dogs' names and comment on the sunrise. Mainly we are quiet, our eyes on the horizon. You don't come for the sunrise then miss it for the other random person.

"Are you down for the week?" he says.

"Actually, I just moved here, a few weeks ago," I reply.

"Amazing. I would love to be able to live here full-time. Ben and Daisy are sure happy to meet."

"Ya."

"How have I not seen you yet if you're a local? I'm here every sunrise, every weekend."

"Oh, I don't do sunrises really. I just had a bad sleep, so…"

"Ahh, makes sense now."

Sometimes playing it cool is your best bet. When I first saw her, down the beach, she looked like a chrysalis in her white wrap, just sitting there on her blanket, her island on a sea of sand. As I neared and could see into her eyes, I wished we didn't have to speak at all.

I find out that she grows things to sell at farmers' markets, and she asks me where home is if it isn't here. I tell her that during the week I work in the city, New York City. I don't want to go, but I probably should. I call to Daisy, "Come on, girl!"

As I am walking away, I have to resist turning back to look at her. She has the air of a caged bird about her. I wonder what happened to her that caused her eyes to be both sad and guarded. And yet. And yet. This changes everything. I had never believed in love at first sight because I'd never seen her. I can actually feel my heart beating. I bend down to pick up a perfectly round, white stone. Next Saturday seems so far away.

As I watch him walk away, I wonder if I will see him again. "He seemed nice, huh, Ben?" No reply.

I shake out my blanket and start for home, stopping to inspect a white pebble. It makes the cut, so I stash it in my pocket. "Home" is a funny word. Usually, I think it takes time for a new place to feel like *home*. But ever since I can remember, I have felt at home here, even though I only spent a week or two here every year. Some places just feel right.

Buying a little beach house here is my dream come true. People say that "sometimes when one door closes, another one opens" because it's true. With the money from my divorce settlement, I was able to move here. I have picked up my dream from where it left off, somewhere in my first year of university, and I am never going to put it on a shelf again.

Ben and I arrive back at the house. I let him inside then head for the outside shower. Every beach house should have one. It's attached to the side of the house and matches it perfectly, yellow with white trim. It's still chilly this early in the season, but hot water solves so much.

I cook Ben and myself scrambled eggs. Yes, I cook for my dog, and why not? After cleaning up, I head out to the greenhouse. My goal in life used to be to live by the ocean and grow things to sell at a farmers' market. And that is exactly what I am doing. Me, by myself. Well, Ben, too, of course. But I don't need anyone else.

The following Saturday he walks her beach again, but well after sunrise, since she said she doesn't usually catch them. As he walks down the sandy path between the dunes, he says a silent prayer for her to be there. He turns right to walk down the beach and sees her. His heart leaps. Ben is sitting beside her on what he is now guessing is her favorite beach blanket.

Her hair is flying in the breeze. As soon as he catches her scent, Ben jumps up and runs straight towards Daisy. Dogs have it easy, he thinks. When Eve turns to look at him, he waves.

As I see him slowly walking down the beach, it surprises me that I feel happy to see him again. I guess I have basically been alone since the beginning of April, and now it is nearly the end of the month. Turning a backyard into a business is a full-time job. I really only need Ben. Although, by the look of it, he is magically in love with Daisy. I wave back to Jamie.

The sunshine is dazzling and the air is crisp. The offshore breeze is making me wish I had a hair elastic. Past the waves, the sea is cobalt and calm. I welcome the crash of every wave. I am never done with it, with this. At this time of year there are almost no people on the beach, leaving it not barren, but boundless.

As he walks towards me, I unwittingly notice his body. He looks like some type of athlete. But what kind? He is tall and I want to say long. He has well-muscled legs and a narrow waist. But from there his body widens into shot-put shoulders. He has bronze-brown, slightly curly hair. I guess his age to be around thirty, definitely older than me by a long shot. Okay fine…he's handsome.

I bet he has an amazing girlfriend back in the city. As he draws near, I find myself checking his ring finger. Not married. I guess my being happy to see him means I need to add *make more friends* to my to-do list, preferably female.

I stand and walk towards the wet sand. We talk about the weather, the dogs, our hometowns.

Safe. Jamie seems like an untroubled soul, peaceful. I had chalked that up to it being sunrise the first time. But again today he strikes me the same way. He doesn't need to fill in the gaps. He is unhurried. Quiet.

Eve took my breath away the first time I met her. As I am walking away from her today, I still feel almost electric. She is mystical and magic. Maybe she always seems a little sad because I always see her staring out to sea. She doesn't flirt with me, and I'm guessing she isn't looking for a relationship. So, I need to take this very slowly. I want her in my arms on her terms. Patience, Jamie, patience.

The following weekend, their paths never cross.

Sit

The next Saturday morning is a little cloudy, but I head to the beach anyway. Offshore and a ways to the south there are ominous dark clouds. Storms are good, they bring the best shells onto the beach. The air smells a little bit like rain, but weather along the coast can change in a minute. That storm might miss us completely and not make landfall until Egg Harbor. Ben and I find our usual spot, and he saunters off to sniff some seaweed. I love that dog. What would I do without him? Touch wood.

I try to stay focused on my book, *The Time Traveler's Wife*[1] (I read it every summer), but I notice

---

[1] *The Time Traveler's Wife* by Audrey Niffenegger time traveled to be in this book.

when Daisy and Jamie are within sight. I decide to continue looking down.

"Hi Eve."

"Hi Jamie."

Daisy and Ben run off to play.

"Looks like a storm's brewing. Mind if I sit?"

When Jamie sits on the blanket, the world shifts. So does the wind, and he thinks he can smell something less briny…her. He takes a deep breath in through his nose and slowly lets it out.

"How's farm life treating you? Did you make a killing at the market last Sunday?"

"Actually, it went really well. I sold almost everything and got a lot of positive feedback from the other vendors."

"I'm happy for you. I have to check it out some time. By habit I always stop at that farm stand, Conovers, just off the parkway, then hit Rick's Seafood in North Wildwood."

They were both quiet for a minute. Eve debated what to say next. Deciding to actually really get to know someone is always a risk. Once you care, it's hard to uncare.

"Jamie, do you have a girlfriend back in the city? Because I wouldn't want you to get the wrong idea. I'm not looking for more than friendship here. I just…"

"Eve, I don't happen to have a girlfriend, no, but that's not what this is. I'm not coming on to you. I imagine we will know each other for the rest of our lives. This is my favorite place on the planet, and I am guessing yours too. Neither of us is probably going anywhere, not for long at least. So we should be friends. Right?"

"Oh…I never thought of it like that. I guess I am always stuck in the moment. Wow, and you had already seen our forever. As friends, I mean."

I love hearing her say "our forever," but this is dangerous territory. So I try to safely navigate us out of it. After a few seconds of silence, I turn the conversation to her.

"So, how did you end up living in Vancouver?"

"My mom lives there. I went to McGill, in Montreal, like my parents, and when my boyfriend said he wanted to live in Vancouver after we graduated, it just seemed like destiny. Boyfriend turned husband...turned ex-husband. We broke up, almost a year ago. I left him. I'm oversharing, huh?"

"No, I want to hear the whole story. That's too bad, having to leave a marriage. Sorry."

"Sorry?"

"Sorry to be commenting on it...on something so personal."

"He was a dick. I'm much happier alone."

I look right at her and say nothing. Suddenly the rain, which had been holding off, gives forth. There's the rumble of thunder and a lightning strike maybe a mile out. We're soaked in seconds.

"Come to my place, it's closer," says Eve. "The beach is no place to be when there's lightning."

My brain leaves me alone as Jamie and I, and the dogs, make a run for it. We enter the screened-in front porch, and I pull beach towels out of the basket by the door.

"I wish I had a fireplace."

"That would be nice," says Jamie, with a little too much emphasis on the "would."

"I'll make tea…or coffee?"

"I like them both. Thank you."

"Great. Come on in."

The rain doesn't seem to be letting up, so I ask Jamie if he wants to throw his drenched clothing into the dryer.

"Are you trying to get me out of my clothes, Miss Eve? I'm shocked."

"No! Wait…what? Ha ha, you're teasing me. Very funny, Jamie." I direct him to the robe hanging on the back of my bedroom door and point out the bathroom.

As Eve heads to the laundry room, I take a look around her place. The outside is pure beach house, and in here it's the same. The line of shells on her walkway continues right up the steps and onto her patio and then just keeps going. There won't be any shells left at this rate. Outside, she has rocks instead of grass. Low maintenance, I like that. Her house is tidy on the inside as well, but cozy. She likes light yellow. By the front door hangs a sign with key hooks. It says "The Nest" and depicts a tiny nest with three robin's eggs. The walls are lined with white bookcases. There are books, yes, but also more shells. The art on the walls is decidedly "beachy," but not at all tacky.

Once in her bedroom, I quickly dry off and try on the robe. I am surprised that it fits! I will just have to ask her about that in around fifteen seconds. Also, I am kind of disappointed. It always looks so cute, in movies, when a guy has to wear a girl's robe. I take note of the maybe ten shell-themed throw pillows on her entirely white and fluffy bed. On her bedside table is a framed photo of Ben.

When I wander into the kitchen, she turns and looks at me. Her eyes go wide.

"I've never seen a man in that."

I am glad she has spoken because I am speechless. She is wearing an old lace cover up over a pale yellow bathing suit. I guess that's what was handy in the laundry room. Then my brain reminds my eyes to look at her face. One of her eyebrows is decidedly raised. She points her thumb over her shoulder, indicating the laundry room. As I walk past her, I think I catch her mouth breaking into a grin.

Thump. She feels her heart leap. She thinks, nope. No, no, no. No, sir. No catching feelings. He is a friend. F-r-i-e-n-d. Period. She fills the kettle and starts a war in her head, where feelings safely belong. The war is about wanting him here and thinking it would be better if he goes. Ben seems perfectly happy all snuggled up with Daisy, like an old married couple. Traitor.

Eve leads Jamie back onto the porch, tea in hand.

"Do all of your cups have shells on them?"

"No, some of them have seagulls."

She safely positions them in the two Adirondack chairs, facing out towards the street, to watch and wait out the storm. He is silently wishing he could magic his tea into a beer. The thought that she seems a little uncomfortable around him leads him to feel both worry and hope. Worry, because what if she is thinking about blocking him out or, worse, just doesn't like him. Hope, because maybe, just maybe, she is afraid to look at him because she is starting to feel something.

Meanwhile, right beside him, the war in my head continues to rage. I peek at him. He is silently watching the rain. I look away. Why does he have to be so handsome? I bet he even smells good. This would be a lot easier if he wasn't so beautiful.

The rain slowly tapers off and surprisingly, the sun comes out.

"Wow, just like that. Huh. Wanna see the backyard? It will be sunnier out there."

"Mmm…smell that petrichor."

"That what the heck?"

"Petrichor. You know, the smell of right now and also just before it starts to rain. It's like a good dirt smell, with a hint of dill and vine-ripened tomatoes. Minerally."

"Oh, you mean what rain smells like. I feel you, the dill thing, maybe also like ozone. Petrichor, eh?"

"It's actually a smell released by freshly rained-on soil, like a fragrance locked in time. Petra for stone, and chor for what flows in the veins of the Greek gods."

"That's very cool."

When they reach the backyard, Jamie wonders at the marvel that is her tiny farm. There's a greenhouse to the left, a chicken coop to the right, four raised planter boxes down the middle, and a small barn and fenced area at the back. The empty "barn" is more just a shelter really, you can see right into it. Encircling it all are highbush blueberry shrubs and maple trees. Multiple hummingbirds are visiting her many feeders.

"This place could use a miniature pony. That would make it perfect."

"I wish."

"I know a guy."

Eve slowly turns her head to look at him.

Jamie feels a spark ignite between them. He looks deeply into her eyes, for the first time, and sees his everything.

She feels it too. What started as the joy of maybe getting a miniature pony has transformed into the heat of staring into his eyes. He is at least a head taller than she is, so his eyes are slightly hooded. She looks away first.

"The Tiny Ranch," he says.

"Huh?"

"The Tiny Ranch. That's the name of my friend's Mom's miniature pony farm. We could ride down there sometime and check it out."

Eve's mind is racing. What's happening here? "No…I mean, thanks, but that's too much of a bother. If I could just, um…have the contact number?"

"Absolutely," I say as we turn and walk back inside. Remember Jamie, give her time. This has to be *her* idea, or it will never happen. If she doesn't choose me, that's fine, as long as she truly knows me. But if she shuts me out before finding out, I know I will have lost something very special, without ever having had a chance.

"It's just before you reach Cape May. I'll call you from home and give you the number." I watch as Eve writes her name and number on a piece of notepaper. There's a panic in her eyes.

"Eve…it's normal for neighbors to share each other's phone numbers. Look, here, I'll write mine down too. Look, now we'll also know each other's last names. See, Jamie Adams at your service. And you are…a Flemming. Eve Flemming, nice to finally meet you."

As he reaches out his hand, I think, don't take it. Also, what if the sparks are visible? I am such a sham. My brain only wants to be friends, but my body is full of other ideas. Now I'm the traitor. I can't just *not* shake his proffered right hand, so I reach my hand out. I say, "I'm not a Flemming." The handshake continues, minus the shaking part. This is lasting far too long and not nearly long enough. We both look down at our linked hands and simultaneously let go. I knew it. Sparks.

"Wait, you aren't?"

"No, Flemming was my married name. I actually like the name, so I just haven't bothered to change it back. My maiden name is Lang."

"Eve Lang, lovely. What are you the day slash night before?"

"My birthday is December 24, actually."

"That's cool. You could have ended up a Noel, or Nic, or Carol…or Holly. I pick Eve too. I am *never* taking an apple from you."

"I have no plans to offer you apples Mr. Adams… ha…ha. Oh, wait, that's kinda creepy. Anyway, if I did try, I am certain that I could tempt you. Easily." Jamie gives me a peculiar smile in response. As he reaches down to pet Daisy, I say, "You love her like I love Ben."

"We humans are funny like that. We know to love our dogs fiercely but not our humans."

"It's because they love us fiercely first. Dogs are great teachers. Also, we know that we won't have them forever."

After Jamie leaves, I resist the urge to smell my robe. When I return to the living room, Ben is staring at me.

"What?"

Nothing.

"Ben, what? He is just a friend. That's it, ok? Ben...stop staring at me like that. You're the only man for me. Come on, I'll make you some dinner. How about salmon and rice with peas?"

I make myself the same thing. After dinner, I run myself a bubble bath and grab *The Time Traveler's Wife*. It's gotten wet at the beach many times, so bringing it into the bath is no big deal. I'm in bed by ten, and I drift off to sleep thinking about the garden.

I wake at 7:30, my resolve renewed! He is a great guy, and I am glad I met him, but my dream is never, ever taking a back seat again. Today is fertilizer day, and I need to start more microgreens. Those sold like hotcakes last Sunday. "What even are hotcakes? Should I have gone into the hotcakes business?" Ben grins up at me; at least someone thinks I'm funny. "I love you Ben. Marry me."

At ten o'clock, a reasonable hour, I call The Tiny Ranch, and I tell Ben that he might be getting a sibling. By eleven, I am all packed up for the market, which runs from twelve to four. Some farmers' markets start early in the day, but church is still sacred around here, so ours has a nice late start.

Towards

Another week passes and I am mostly successful in not thinking about Jamie. I make it to the beach most mornings and sometimes return to enjoy it in the late afternoon. But, by Thursday, I can't help noticing how Ben rushes through the dunes to get to the beach, then turns his entire body to the left, looking for Daisy. I know they won't be here until Saturday, and even then there's no guarantee.

I can't lie to myself. I am kind of looking forward to seeing Jamie again. He is one of my only friends around here, so far. I'm excited to tell him about my visit to The Tiny Ranch. I loved the little brown mini. His name is actually "Brownie." I just have to fix up his little barn, mend the fence, and get hay and grain, then I can bring him home. The owner only charged me two hundred dollars because I am a friend of Jamie's. Plus, Brownie isn't a young pony, so he would have been a hard sell. He's adorable. Telling Jamie about him will be really exciting.

It's been a long week. I love my job but sometimes counseling troubled teens weighs heavily on my soul. By Thursday morning I decide to take Friday off and head down to the shore early. I have thought about Eve so many times this week. I see her on the inside of my eyelids when I am trying to sleep. Then I fall asleep and dream about her! I wonder what it would be like to hold her in my arms, to kiss her.

I arrive at the beach at 10 a.m. Daisy bounds ahead of me and, sure enough, here comes Ben. Just as I look right, I see Eve standing up. This time she walks towards me. Progress.

I can't believe my eyes. Wait. What? It's only Friday. I am on my feet and moving towards Jamie before I even know it. It just happened. I am happy and wonder about my appearance. Then I remember to curb my enthusiasm. Wait, no, I do get to be excited because I have miniature pony news!

"Hi."

"Hi."

He looks right into my eyes and I have to look away. I watch Ben and Daisy for a few seconds. When I feel brave enough, I turn back to see that he is still looking straight at me.

"How's it going? You're a day early, eh?"

"Not happy to see me, Eve?"

"No, I mean, yes…I just meant, like, that you usually only come down on Saturday."

"No, Eve, I am actually here on Friday nights. When you see me Saturday morning, I have in fact slept in my own very nearby bed."

The thought of Jamie in a bed makes me light-headed. I must be sure not to picture that again, ever. But I'm single, not a saint. Am I blushing? Shit.

"So, since I am here early, I thought maybe you could use some company. I know I could. It seems silly for you and I to be eating dinner alone, two miles apart. Cooking is kind of a hobby of mine. What do you say?"

Blank air.

"It's just dinner, Eve."

Am I breathing? Time isn't behaving properly. "Are you still not coming on to me?"

"Eve…I get the feeling that you are not ready for dating. So, no, I am not 'coming on' to you. But, to be honest, I find you to be exceedingly beautiful." The most beautiful woman I have ever seen. She's intoxicating. Her way of quietly staring at the waves lets me know that we are a match made in heaven. Getting rained on last week actually made her laugh! Can she see all of these feelings in my eyes? Uh oh. She is just staring at me. I slowly place my hands on her shoulders. This is my first time touching her, other than our handshake. I look at her lips. Start talking, Jamie.

"Eve. You okay?"

"What? Yes. I just…ummm…wow, you just called me beautiful."

"You are beautiful. It's just a fact, Eve. I am sure many men have told you that. But the fact remains that we are just friends. So, as friends, let's make dinner together. You can be my 'mise en place' girl. My chop-bitch."

His use of the term "chop-bitch" finally breaks me out of the Jamie-said-I-am-beautiful spell. I laugh out loud, then playfully push him. "Jamie Adams, I am nobody's bitch."

"Is that a yes? I want to hit Rick's before they run out of the good stuff."

"Which is?"

"Soft-shell crabs, of course. And I'll pick up some of their coleslaw."

"They sell a hot sauce called Hank Sauce. I love the Cilanktro one. Have you ever tried it?"

"Why, madame, I have indeed. That's my secret ingredient for serving crab. I dredge them in a flour and Old Bay mix, sauté them in a pan, then serve them with melted Cilanktro-butter. Corn would be the perfect side, but, since we don't have that yet, corn fritters will have to do. Have I convinced you yet?"

"It is a wonder we never met sooner. We like the same places. Maybe we've even been in Rick's together one time?"

We never have. I would remember ever having seen her before. I am just glad we have met now. She isn't ready for me, but I am one hundred percent ready for her.

"Are we in yes-ville yet?"

"Yes, I believe friends eat amazing food together all of the time. Besides, Ben has the super hots for Daisy. He would kill me if he knew I'd denied him an evening to cement their undying love. Maybe they can share a noodle."

"Great. What time can I expect you?"

"What time do you want me?"

Her words catch me off guard. I blink slowly, regain my composure, and hope that she didn't notice the pause. "My place at sunset? There's a great view from the bay near me."

"Okay, see you then. Can I bring anything?"

"Just you, that's everything." Wow…my mouth just does whatever it wants. "Well, and Ben, of course. Are you okay with me plying you with liquor? I'm a beer guy, mainly, but I like white wine with crab."

"Ply away. I love white wine."

"Okay."

We part ways and I feel like pumping my fist in the air. Eve is coming to dinner at my place. I have to remember to take this slow.

Bolt

My mind is reeling. Jamie called me beautiful. Wow. And now we are having dinner together. Friend. Friend. Friend. I take my time with my appearance, a rare event. I don't get out much. Scott faulted me for being an introvert, but honestly, I am my happiest when my hands are in the dirt and the only sounds I hear are seagulls and the waves in the distance. I am wearing my favorite Levi's and a loose white V-neck sweater. I add a necklace with a tiny gold octopus pendant and a spritz of Cinnabar perfume, and I am good to go. Sandals? Nah…flip-flops.

I'm a little worried about tonight, but I haven't had any grown-up fun in a long time. I deserve a fun night, to let my hair down a little. I arrive half an hour before sunset. Jamie's house is beautiful. What does he do for a living? My family used to have a bay house, my grandmother anyway. Daisy barks twice as she sees us walking up the sidewalk. Then, Jamie is there. His eyes start at my face, run down my body—my now tingling body— then return to my face.

"Hi."

"Hi yourself. These are some sweet digs you got here."

Jamie looks left, then right. "Where's your truck?"

"Oh. I walked. I would never drink and drive, not even in a tiny beach town off season."

"I agree, but that's quite a walk in flip-flops. Come in. This place has been in my family for generations. I didn't have to buy it and the mortgage is paid off. So, it's just taxes and upkeep really. I can fix most things myself. One day I want to be able to live here year-round. But, for now… gotta pay the bills."

Jamie gives me a tour of the main floor of the house. He has lots of family photos. There are at least three photos of a woman who I am guessing is his mom. When I reach the bookcase under the stairs, I see another photo of her. It's one of those old-time black and whites with the cheek tint added after. I pick it up, then Jamie confirms that it's his mother. He goes on to tell me that she died when he was ten years old.

"That's so sad."

"It was then. But a lot of time has gone by. I had a great dad, still do. Let's grab a beer and head out to the dock. Any preferences?"

"Do you have Heineken?"

"That's my favorite beer, so yes I do."

When we walk out the door, I am greeted by the smell of the bay. He has a covered back patio and a floating dock with a boat slip. It's almost high tide, so the barnacles aren't visible and the sometimes overwhelming smell of bays is not just bearable but actually pleasant.

"Earlier today, you said house 'near the bay,' but you actually live smack on the bay." I turn to look at him, but he's already looking at me. "Cheers," he says. We clink cans. "This looks like a good one, a few clouds to spice it up." We head down to the dock and sit in his impeccable, red Adirondack chairs (mine are plastic). I'm not much for chatting during sunsets, so I am relieved when he also doesn't feel the need to have a conversation while experiencing the glory. However, I do have exciting news, so I break form.

"Guess what?" He looks over at me. "I went and looked at the pony Rebecca had at The Tiny Ranch. His name is Brownie. I loved him and he loved me and soon he will be mine. Thanks for the lead."

"That's great news for him too."

"What do you mean?"

"I mean he just won the lottery in the owner department. I know that you'll love him like crazy. I see how you are with Ben, and even Daisy. Heck, you love your chickens."

"I think I'm the one who won. Thanks for the connection."

"My pleasure."

We finish watching the sunset, mostly in silence. As the sun drops below the horizon, the seagulls cry their farewells. The sky is layers of creamsicle orange, robin's-egg blue, fuchsia-red, mirrored on the surface of the bay. Rainbow ripples.

The bay, placid yet full of hidden power. The ancestral smell of mist and marshes, like melting snow, like a memory.

"Why do seagulls seem to love sunsets? They never fail to dance around in front of a colorful sky or peacefully watch from the rooftops. Seagulls love sunsets as much as people do, I'm sure of it," I say.

"Mmm…I never really thought about it. Now that I have, I think you're right. They're very 'worshipy' about it. It's cool."

"'Worshipy,' eh? I'm pretty sure that's not a word."

"It is now. Speaking of worshipping…are you ready to be amazed at and astounded by my culinary prowess?"

"That's a lot of hype, good sir. But yes, I am near starving."

Jamie pours us each a glass of wine and installs me on a barstool on the other side of the kitchen's open high counter. My job is more to watch him than help him, which is fine by me. He expertly sautés the soft-shell crabs, plops corn fritter batter into his deep fryer, and removes the coleslaw from the fridge. After preparing his melted Cilanktro butter, he comes around the counter and sits right next to me. I am so relieved to not be sitting across from each other, face to face. This feels more casual, buddy like.

"Not bad, eh?" he says, gently nudging me with his elbow.

"Wow, nice use of the 'eh,' and this is so good. Honestly, I would be ecstatic to get this in a restaurant."

"I think I even heard a little 'mmmmm-ing.' Very cute."

"Oh, sorry."

"Sorry for what?"

"Oh, my ex hated when I did that."

"I'm not him."

"Thank God."

"So, what happened there, if you don't mind my asking?"

"Well, some of it's hard to talk about…"

"I'm a pretty good listener."

"Umm…well, the short version, and I want to give the short version because the past is behind me. The short version is that when I needed him most, he wasn't there for me. We…I…had a miscarriage, at five months…"

"Oh, Eve."

"I was having a hard time after, and he was just like 'get over it.' But I didn't have a choice in the matter. I had anxiety and felt depressed. My sleeping was messed up. I was crying one day and he got mad at me. In the heat of the moment, he said he was glad we weren't having a baby. He said he realized when I was no longer 'any fun'—because ya, pregnant—that he actually wanted our old life back. Just the two of us, our date nights. He said maybe this was a blessing."

"Did you slap him?"

"I slapped him so hard, he actually put his hand on his cheek. He walked out the door, slammed it, and drove off. Slapping him sort of woke me up. I wasn't getting better because he wasn't caring for me. My soul hurt. He just wasn't a nurturing person. So, I guess it is better to not have him as the father of my child. I can never unwish that baby though."

As a tear slides down her face, I so badly want to pull her into my arms, but I'm not sure how she would react, so I let the space between us remain. Silence seems like the best solace. Eve takes a deep breath and continues.

"So, I left him. I moved in with my mom for a bit, got better, made plans. And here I am."

"Wow. You've been through a lot." Now I understand why she seemed a little broken. Why she just can't see that a better man is standing right in front of her.

As we finish tidying up, Jamie suggests we take the dogs for an evening beach walk.

"Sure, that puts me home early enough to get a good night's sleep."

"In that case, tough luck, Daisy girl. No walk for you. It's too early to call it a night."

Jamie pours us another glass of wine as I wander back to the bookcase. There's too much Hemingway here for my taste. But there are a few goodies and even a couple of my top tens. *One Hundred Years of Solitude* is there, it's magical butterflies safely hidden between the pages. Also *Beloved*, by Toni Morrison, and *Braveheart*, by Randall Wallace. And, best of all, the complete works of Albert Camus.

"Need a good book?"

"You a big Hemingway guy?"

"No. I've read them, but my dad's the big fan. I think it was that generation's thing. I am more of a Russian lit fan."

"Me too. *Anna Karenina*, right?"

"Absolutely."

"But I can't get through *War and Peace*. Every time I try, I die by page 231. I'm reincarnated, grow up, try to read *War and Peace*, and boom, die by page 231."

"You're funny, Eve. As a strange coincidence, I have also started it but never finished it. Maybe no one has ever finished it. People who claim they have are just lying about it."

"They must be."

By 10 p.m., I am pretty tipsy and know it is time to get going. Ben and Daisy look ready for a sleepover, but I'm not. Or *am* I? Jamie is definitely a very attractive man. And he did say I was beautiful.

"You know earlier, on the beach…"

"Yeah…"

"You said I prolly heard that I was beautiful all the time…but, I didn't, I haven't. My mom, maybe, but not guys. Even Scott only ever said I looked 'pretty,' and then only if I was wearing makeup. In my teens, I spent most of my time in ballet classes, so, ya, I don't have a lot of history with guys. Just Scott. And as we both know…"

In unison: "He was a dick."

"I'm the first man that has ever called you beautiful? Wait, were you a virgin before Scott?"

"Wow, wine really loosens you up, eh, Jamie? Geez."

"Sorry."

"It's fine. And yes, I was. What a dork."

"I think it's sweet."

"You're sweet." Did I just say that?

"Do friends kiss?"

"No, Jamie!"

"You're right, sorry. I like you. I'm trying to stick to the plan, just friends, but to be honest, I'm finding it really hard here. Let's just kiss and see if there's any chemistry? Then, we can just move on with our lives."

"Jamie, no. I don't see a man in my life. I let one get in the way of my dreams once already." I stand up, literally trying to stand my ground, but I am apparently on a slippery slope because my whole entire brain is playing a romantic dream sequence in which Jamie is kissing me. My eyes are closed when I feel his hands on my shoulders. I open my eyes, and he is there.

"I'm sorry, Eve. Evie. But I have to know. I'll go slow, meet me halfway or don't."

I know I am already lost. The closer he gets, the nearer I want him. As promised, he stops halfway. I close the gap. Right before our lips meet, I take a deep breath, open my mouth, and let out all of the air. And then he kisses me. I breathe in fast through my nose. Cue music. Our kiss is a dozen raised glazed donuts and all of the Fourth of July fireworks. Our bodies flash colors like an octopus, but slower, like a mood ring. Suddenly I feel his hands pressing against the sides of my head. Double thump. What am I doing?! No, no, no. I pull away.

"That can never happen again. It's prolly just the wine. I should get going. I'm gonna go, right now. Thanks for dinner. Really, no harm, no foul. We both did that. But let's go back to just being friends. Right. Okay. Come on, Ben. Goodbye…Jamie."

Wait

"Hello."

"Hi, Dad. Got a minute?"

"For you, I have a lifetime of minutes, son. What's wrong?"

"I think I messed something up. Something important. I met this girl, a few weeks back, out here. On the beach, in fact. She's…I don't know…she's special. We've talked a few times, and last night she came over for dinner. Long story short, I kissed her. She has said to me before that she just wants to be friends, but I feel so much chemistry between us. There's a spark there, I'm sure of it. But, after the kiss thing, she bolted. She literally walked straight out the door. What do I do?"

"Hmmm, son. Why did you kiss a woman who said she just wanted to be friends?"

"She left her husband about a year ago. So, I really thought she just thought she wasn't ready, but maybe she is? The way it came up, I leaned in and said, 'let's just see if there's a spark, if no spark, at least we don't have to wonder anymore.' The thing is, Dad, when I leaned in, she did too. She kissed me back. Then she bolted."

"Jamie…you might not want to hear this, but it's the truth. There's nothing you can do. You have to wait. Let her be the one to come to you. She leaned in, so it's in her to want you. Her bolting is the surest sign there is that she felt something. That's why she's afraid. That's the good news. The waiting is the hard part."

"You always know just what to say to me. I feel a lot better. Okay, ya, I can do that. I can wait. Thanks, Dad. You good?"

"I am well, son, and you're welcome. Take care. See you next week."

"I love you, Dad. Bye."

☆

I could hardly sleep last night. What was I thinking? I kissed him back, ugh, dammit. I'm weak. I spent this whole year working on myself and learning to be strong, alone, and in just a few weeks I've let the first guy I've met slip right in the door. Hello, come on in, make yourself at home. My heart is a piñata, here— want a stick? I guess I don't know how to be just his friend. Maybe it's best if I just avoid him, at least until I figure this out.

Love Love

"Hi, Mom."

"Hello, sweetie. How are things?"

"I just need to talk, maybe I need some advice? I'm not sure. After Dad left, you decided you didn't need a man. I want to be strong, like you. I got burned by Scott and I don't want that to happen again."

"Did something happen, Eve?"

"Sorry, right, context. I set up this life here, and I'm happy. I love it. So along comes this neighbor, he lives closer to 96th Street, Jamie, and in just a few weeks he managed to get my guard down. I've been avoiding him for a while now, but I have…feelings or some dumb thing. I can avoid him, physically…like, geographically…but, my mind turns to him constantly."

"Okay, honey. First off, it's okay to be wary of a man. Does he seem like a good person?"

"Yes, truly."

"Then here it is, baby. You're one hundred percent wrong about me. I didn't make some decision to never let a man in after your Dad left us. I was busy with you and work, and now I have my work, my volunteering, and my friends. I have the dogs and stacks of books I still want to read. I just don't feel the need to date. My life feels full. Lastly…I truly did love your father. He was the love of my life. I can't explain it, but there it is. I haven't wanted another. But, baby, if I did meet someone, someone I couldn't stop thinking about, I would fall happily into it. And this 'no men for me' policy is fine right after a break-up, but it's not meant to last forever. It's just not who you are. Remember how you used to say that you love love? That's the true you. Don't you dare let Scott have taken that away from you."

"Wow. Why did I never ask you about this before? I really thought you *decided* not to let a man in, like it was safer that way."

"Safer isn't always better."

"Oh my gosh, I feel like a fool. I tried to carve out a new world view as a *reaction* to Scott."

"I think your Dad leaving us is part of it too, right? Trust issues?"

"Shit. You're right. I have to go, Mom. There's someone I need to talk to. If it's not too late."

After hanging up, I try to figure out what to say to Jamie. I will my fingers to dial his number on my phone, but I can't decide the right thing to say. It was probably just the wine. Honestly, he hasn't even tried to get in touch with me since then. Maybe he didn't like kissing me, or maybe he doesn't like freaks who bolt out doors. I can hardly blame him. Sigh.

I Spy

Knock, knock, knock.

I press open the door and he's just standing there. Jamie. He's holding a nest cupped between both of his hands. I am speechless. He slowly extends the nest to me.

"I'm sorry I kissed you. Here, this is for you. I found it. Please let's go back to being friends."

"Okay," I say, while taking the intricately woven nest out of his hands.

"I can't promise not to want more, but...did you say okay?"

"Yes."

Blink, blink. "Can friends hug?"

"Is this another chemistry quiz?"

"No."

"Then, yes."

I think this is the best hug of my entire life. Jamie smells like sunshine and feels like soft rain...and also like a giant tree that thinks that I am very worthy of embracing. Jamie thinks that I just want to be friends, and that is good. I want to do this on my own terms, if at all. I want to really, really know him before my heart gets all tangled up in feelings and emotions. But, it's going to be hard. Seeing him at my door, I allowed myself to really *see* him. He has to be the most gorgeous man in the world. There must be broken hearts lying dead on the ground all over New York City. Those poor girls.

She let me back in! That was a lot easier than I'd expected. I gave her some space, and today, I was just going to hand her the nest, say sorry, and leave. Hey, this is a great hug. She smells like sexy cinnamon. Don't start rubbing her back. Let go first, be the one...nope.

I was doing what Dad had said, but then I started to wonder, what if she thinks the kiss hadn't been good for me, or that her avoiding me didn't matter to me? Hey, this hug is my new normal... aaand she stopped. A kaleidoscope of small white butterflies floats out the door.

"Where's Daisy?"

"In the car."

"I'll bring Ben out to say hi."

The dogs show all of the joy that I am feeling. I wonder how Eve feels.

"Do you want to go for a walk?"

"Sure."

Eve and Jamie walk, side by side, dogs trotting ahead, the two blocks to the beach. Leaving their flip-flops by the greyed fence protecting the dunes, they head towards the surf's edge, turning south. The wind is low. Flocks of tiny intrepid sandpipers bravely run towards the water, change their minds, and beat a hasty retreat. They walk for more than a mile, pointing out the best shells along the way, but leaving them where the ocean has placed them. They reach the point at sunset and gaze at the sky to the west of their little island, their hands nearly touching, the intricate channels and estuaries beyond them, unseen but felt. Behind them, waves are slamming onto the sand, kicking up mist. They peek at each other but say nothing, both sensing that they are fragile, like porcelain, like silence, like hearts. The sun is in a constant state of rising and setting, over, and over, and over, somewhere between yesterday and tomorrow, like the keys to time.

As they head back, Eve asks Jamie about his mom.

"There's not much to tell. When I was ten, she got cancer. I have a few special memories, Christmases, things like that. Then she's just gone. I think I was mad all the way up to my twenties. Tell me about your dad; you only ever mention your mom."

"Well, I was also ten, so my mom didn't tell me everything then, just that they were getting a divorce and he was going to be living in Europe. I gave up wishing he would visit me after I was sixteen. I'd seen him less than once a year. He didn't even call me on my birthdays after the first few years. He's a pilot. Turns out that while he was away for work, he was also cheating on my mom. The woman is ten years younger than my mom. She got pregnant, and my dad told my mom he wanted a divorce. She made him tell her the whole story. They live in France. He has never reached out to me, like, even for me to meet my little brother. I just recently found out from my mom that one of the reasons she never married again is because, even though it was only true for her, he was the love of her life."

Saturday morning Jamie arrives and, as planned, after his sunrise beach walk with Daisy, we have a coffee together. Ben and Daisy have the pleasure of seeing what the other one smells like early in the morning.

"Good morning, Sunshine! I brought you a twirly unicorn shell."

"An eastern auger, though your name is pretty cute."

We bring our shell-mug coffees, milk no sugar, to my front porch. The sky is still glowing from the sun's exertion of rising, while maintaining epic standards of beauty.

"More people starting to clog up the beach, eh?" I say.

"'Tis the season, but it's fine; September will arrive before you know it, then it's practically a ghost town."

"I can't wait to experience the off season."

"It's beautiful here all year round. Sometimes we get whales off the coast in winter and seals right on the beach."

"So cool."

"The eeriest thing…that buzzing sound you hear at night, crickets or katydids, maybe both…well, one day it just stops, boom."

"Why?"

"The first frost kills them all."

"Oh, that's actually kind of sad."

"Nature."

Crushed and Cherished

Sunday afternoon finds me at my farm stand, which is covered, thankfully, because it is as hot as heck. The mushroom pâtés are all sold out, and I'm down to my last jar of tomato-jalapeño jelly. Once it's gone, I will probably pack up early. Jamie crossed my mind roughly fifty million times today. I wonder what he's up to. Fishing or working on his near perfect body. Actually, perfect, his body is perfect. He makes me feel like a waif next to him.

I'm going to stop by Rick's and grab a hundred cherrystone clams to make chowder tonight. It's much better the second day, but I can never wait, so I just make a shit ton of it. No clam chowder has ever gone to waste in my fridge.

When I pull up to my house, I see Jamie on my porch. Ben leaps over me to get out of the truck and runs to see Daisy just as Jamie opens the door to the porch. Their reunion is serenaded by doves dancing overhead, no cupids because everyone knows those aren't real.

"Howdy, neighbor."

"Hi."

"I was just passing by and decided to stop by and say hey."

"Where are you headed?"

"Headed back. I was just out sailing with a buddy of mine. I'm not seeing clients tomorrow, so I decided to stay here tonight rather than head back to the city."

"Maybe you want to help me make my famous clam chowder? Manhattan-style, of course."

"Are you in need of a chop-bitch, Miss Evie?"

"Evie?"

"Yes, you are an 'Evie' if ever I've met one... though, I have not."

"If scrubbing a hundred clams, steaming them, reserving the liquid, removing them from their shells, and chopping them makes you my chop-bitch, then yes. But, I shall call you my assistant because I am classy like that."

"Well, since you have given me a promotion, how can I refuse?"

Jamie helps me carry in the Rick's bag and a six of Heineken, and over the next two hours we craft chowder together, the Rolling Stones on the stereo."

"You're a Stones fan," he states rather than asks.

"How can you tell?"

"You can't stop half dancing while you cook, and I see you moving your lips like you know every word. What else do you like?"

"Oh, I only go in for bands that start with the word 'the': The Rolling Stones, The Beatles, The Cure, The Cars, The Clash….The The."

"You're a strange one, Eve, but I like it."

As Jamie is setting the table, he notices my fishbowl full of white stones. He stares at it a little longer than necessary and I wonder what's up there.

"This is the best clam chowder I have ever tasted. It's amazing. What's the secret?"

"It's from *The Summer Shack* cookbook, but I add extra thyme, oregano, garlic, and a splash of Cilanktro. Then I blend it 'til it's almost smooth and throw in some fresh corn when serving. Frozen works in a pinch."

After dinner we grab a beer and head out to see Brownie. It's early evening and the sunset is just beginning.

"The air smells like rain tonight…petrichor, right?"

"Right. What's the trick to getting the little fella to come over to the fence?"

"Oh, here, I tucked some apple chunks into my pocket, go ahead and open the gate. We can walk right in."

Brownie walks right up to Jamie and munches apples from his outstretched hand while Jamie pats his little back.

"Wow, he is killer cute."

"I know. I love him."

Once we are back inside, Jamie asks me about the stones. He tells me that he does the same thing, but he imagines it's for different reasons.

"I don't know why. It's just automatic," I say. "I guess maybe it's part superstition, like I think they're good luck. And part that they represent hope? What about you?"

"Mine's a little sad, but it doesn't make me feel sad. I sort of like to think they represent my mom. Like every time I see one, it's a visit from her. But then, well, I can't just *leave* it there."

"That's beautiful, Jamie."

"You're beautiful."

"So are you."

"Eve…are you coming on to me?"

I laugh. "You wish."

"Wanna hold hands? Just like the kiss test. Don't look at me like that! Hear me out. Let's just hold hands and see what happens. We can do the experiment on the patio if that's easier for you… separate chairs."

"Are you insane?"

"No. Listen, we'll just hold hands for one full minute and if one of us wants to let go, then it's over."

"Okay," I say.

"Really? Okay, let's go."

I follow him out onto the porch, and we sit facing towards the ocean. The seagulls are singing their love songs to the sunset. I look over at Jamie. His one dimple is showing. His head is tilted down and a little to the side. He literally looks mischievous as he holds out his hand. I take it.

"Jamie, do you just want to talk about what happened with the kiss? Clear the air? Do you have questions for me? Because I might be ready to answer them, and then I'll have one for you."

"Can we keep holding hands?"

"Yes."

"Why did you run? Please say that you felt something for me but were just afraid. But if the truth is that you couldn't see the sparks flying, please at least say that I'm a good kisser."

Over the next fifteen minutes I tell Jamie all about my phone call with my mom. I end with the part about not letting Scott take away dating and relationships from me. And then I tell him the truth.

"It was an amazing kiss, for me. It scared me actually. My body revved up to, like, 110 miles per hour in three seconds. Our kiss was a Porsche."

"Perhaps we should have a replay, only minus the running away."

"I'm still afraid, Jamie. Not of you, no, but of getting hurt, yes. My mom reminded me that it's okay to get hurt, but not blindly. You have to believe in something to find it. It's just…I wasn't looking. I'm not ready? No, I'm afraid you won't want me in the end. It's like I don't want to lose you, so I can't have you. Does that make any sense?"

"Come here."

In one smooth move, Jamie slowly pulls me to standing, then right into his embrace. "I never plan on hurting you, Eve. I don't know what the future will bring, but I feel that we could be good together. I want to be the love you believed in before Scott."

"Let's stop saying his name, right?"

"I agree. Forever. Forever no more Scott."

"You said it again."

"I did…sorry 'bout that."

We pull apart a little, but our arms are still behind each other's backs.

"Well," I say, "this was my question before, and it applies even more now. Jamie, why are you so, so…good? What has happened to make you this way? It's like you have a quiet wisdom, like you figured out the secret to being a human. You make me believe that maybe someday I will be ready for happily-ever-after."

"It makes me *very* happy to hear you say that, Eve. And I think I know what you're asking me. Here's the answer. My father once told me, years after my mother had died, that all great stories are actually love stories, because in the end, that's all there is. When I was old enough, he described my mom's last hours. She was on a lot of morphine, so not in a ton of pain, and she just kept saying 'I love you,' over and over."

"That's so special."

"He also told me, quite recently, to let you come to me. That it would be the only way. I've been trying to give you space and time…heh, I'm trying to give you physics, Evie. But, with me gone all week, when I finally do see you, I just feel like we should pack so much into the weekend."

And then she kisses me. Not a Disney movie kiss either; this is another race car kiss. We stay like this for at least five minutes, my hands moving slowly up and down her back and hers pressing against my chest. Then I kiss her chin, her eyes, her cheeks, the corner of her mouth, her nose, until she starts giggling, then back to the races. I am both found and lost.

As I am climbing into bed tonight, the phone rings in the kitchen. It's Jamie.

"Good night, Evie. Thanks for tonight. If you're feeling scared about us, I could come back over and read you a story or something."

"Good night, Jamie."

"You had me at 'hi.'"

I fall asleep wondering what he meant by that and remembering what it felt like to be in his arms…crushed and cherished.

Changing Tides

The following weekend, after talking on the phone daily during the week, Jamie and I decided to play "couple" and see how it goes—kind of an extension of the hand holding game. Little did I know how much I would enjoy this new chapter in our story.

I roll into town at 7:30 p.m., having survived the maniacs and traffic on the drive down. People from Philly and New York City love New Jersey. They complain about it so *you* won't show up at their favorite beach, or worse, drag your sunburnt shoobie ass into Fred's Tavern on Saturday night. Atlantic City is not my favorite place, but most of the other shore towns are amazing, and the powdery sand beaches are stellar. Now forget you ever heard that. It's 7:45 when I arrive at Eve's house.

At 7:45, I finally hear Jamie's car on the rocks of the driveway. I feel both nervous and excited. I take a deep breath and open the door, and because we are playing "couple" this weekend, I run straight into his arms. It is meant to be playful and dramatic, but it actually feels great. More couples should play act overly romanticized reunion scenes. He joins in the fun and swings me around in three circles. It doesn't happen in slow motion, but go ahead and picture it that way, I just did.

"Evie, Vi-Vi," he says, and tentatively kisses me. He lets Daisy out of the car, and she and Ben share their own slow-motion reunion, *Chariots of Fire* soundtrack and all.

"I brought Back Bay crab cakes."

"Oh my gosh, yay! I love how they come in real clam shells. I have fresh corn and a huge beefsteak tomato to go with."

"Perfect, I'm starving. You look so good…I could eat you up. Are those something other than flip-flops on your feet? I didn't know you ever wore anything else. I was looking forward to watching you navigate winter in them."

"I own other kinds of shoes, Jamie. Flip-flops are just my favorite. I put these sandals on for you. It's not very often I bother trying."

"Your hair even looks special. Like a twisty crown made of hair. But I like you every way. You look perfect with or without trying."

Eve opens wine, pours me a glass, and commands me to sit. "Wildfire" is playing on the radio. As she starts to cook, she sings along. Eve hands me four ears of corn to shuck. I have the pleasure of watching the woman I love slice tomatoes while belting out the lyrics to "Wildfire." Clearly, a song about a girl braving a winter storm to find her lost pony speaks to her. She stops singing to check on the crab cakes in the oven, then starts back in. She sways to the music and lifts her chin. She is wearing one of those halter dresses that are really glorified aprons. It's yellow, my favorite color on her. She belts out the last, drawn out "Wildfire," eyes tight shut, then looks right at me and smiles. "God, I love that song," she says.

We eat dinner at the table, which is neither in the kitchen nor in the dining room because it's all the same room. She had to remove a few shells, shocking, and a mason jar of daisies so we could make room for plates and the candle she has taken off the bookshelf. It brings me joy to see her this way, so different from that first morning on the beach. Underneath that joy is a serious desire to untie her halter dress, skip dinner, and run my hands all over her. No way, buddy, not gonna happen. Cool yer jets. Slow and steady wins the race.

Dinner was amazing, and Jamie does the dishes while I check on all of the animals. I've added bunnies recently and saying goodnight to them is my new favorite ritual. Later, we take the dogs for a late-night walk on the beach, then head back to my place for a nightcap. As we walk away from the beach, he takes my hand.

At my front door, he turns me around and steps closer. My back pushes softly against the door as he gently kisses me, then harder as he presses into me, deepening the kiss. I'm swept away, lost at sea. As he pulls away from me, a storm passes over his face. His eyes are a lightning strike on the ocean, steel blue, white hot.

"Is this okay?" he says.

"Don't stop."

"I think we better slow down, Eve."

I know he is wrong but want to let him honor his honor. So we go inside, grab two glasses and a bottle of Baileys, and return to the porch to rate our progress in the "game" of pretending to be a couple. Ben and Daisy curl up at our feet, nose to nose.

"Spend the night."

"What?"

"We don't have to do anything, no more tests, just stay."

"I'm not sure that's a good idea, Eve. I don't want to rush things."

"We could just cuddle, not even naked."

"Vee…you're killing me here. How can I resist you?"

"You can't…it's settled."

So, after more than one but less than seven glasses of Baileys, Jamie and I climb into bed together for the first time. We talk 'til 3 a.m. I awaken before him, so I slip out of bed to use the bathroom, then sneak back under the covers, gently resting my hand on his shoulder.

"Good morning, Vi-Vi."

"Wait. Are you up? Were you already up before me?"

"Of course I was. I'm an early riser, remember? That's how we met," he says, turning to look at me. "I took Ben and Daisy to watch the sunrise, they shared a moment. Then I came back here, got back into bed, and creepily stared at you for a while. You make little meowing sounds in your sleep. I finally decided to try and catch a few more winks. Come here." He wraps his right arm around me, and I snuggle up close to his side. My thoughts turn into wildflowers in my mind. I am all things beautiful. Then my hand, sensing I have stopped manning the ship, gets a mind of its own and starts roving.

"Is this okay?"

"Eve, I was being gallant last night, not rushing you, but if you want more, I have a whole lot more to give you. You just say the word."

"I'm not sure there are words for what I want. I also feel like there are possibilities beyond my imagination."

"This is pretty racy talk Vi. You surprise me."

"Hey, no, I'm not talking about sex positions here, or not mainly. I'm trying to share my feelings, like how I feel about you, this…us."

Her saying *us* does something to me. I roll on top of her, careful not to crush her. I kiss her, then roll back, and she is on top now. She stops kissing me, looks straight into my eyes, and slides her knees up along the sides of my body. Cannons fire. We are both wearing underwear, but we are nevertheless practically having sex. She sits up, grabs the bottom edge of my T-shirt, and as I do a half sit-up, she pulls it over my head and tosses it to the floor. Then her hands go to her own shirt, she grabs the hem, purses her lips, and slowly lifts the pale pink fabric. Her hair cascades over her breasts. She looks like a goddess. I don't know how far she wants to take this, but I am getting harder by the second. As if to answer my question, she slowly starts moving her hips forwards and backwards.

"Vi?"

"Yes."

"Do you want me to touch you? We don't have to go all the way, but you seem, well, if you don't mind my saying, you seem pretty horny."

"I haven't had sex in over a year, Jamie, and…no one has ever, um, 'touched' me."

Wordlessly, I roll Eve onto her back and place my hand on her stomach. I look into her eyes to make sure she wants this as much as I do. She does. I slowly slide my hand down, then into her adorable light yellow Calvin Klein underwear.

A few miles out, and a hundred miles below the surface, the Earth registers a 3.0 quake, thanks to Eve.

When I open my eyes, Jamie has quite the smug look on his beautiful tanned face.

He says, "I want to start everyday doing that for you. Are you blushing? You don't need to be shy around me, Evie."

Then, for who knows what reason, I am crying, not hard, but still. He asks me what's wrong, and I truthfully say that I don't know.

"I just, I…I just feel so many feelings all of a sudden, and maybe I'm a little scared?"

"You're fine; come here, let me hold you. You're just learning for the first time that being intimate releases a lot of emotions. Yeah?"

He's right. I nod my head.

Later that day, as Jamie and I walk the beach, picking up white stones to give each other, we share our histories regarding this particular stretch of sand and our undying devotion to it. I know that I am falling for him. I remind myself that it's okay to love someone even if it might not work out. It's worth the sorrow after to feel the care and desire now. I'm not deeply in love, but I am strongly in like. Also, if I don't have sex with him soon, I might die.

His love for this beach comes from his memories of coming here with his mom. He explains that the light, the sounds, the feel of the sand, the rainbow baby clams, all of it reminds him of her, of how it felt to be ten years old and unencumbered. It reminds him of life pre-grief. But more than that, this has always been his place to escape the city, and even though it's changing year by year, it still feels sacred. Out on fishing boats as a kid, his dad, a marine biologist and conservationist at the New York Aquarium, taught him all about the animals of the coast and the deep sea.

"My dad says that my mom used to love to just sit and stare at the ocean, quietly watching wave after wave. You do that too, Eve. I love that about you."

I tell Jamie about my childhood memories of this place, making drip castles, riding bikes with new friends, getting fudge, floating around the bay on an old surfboard, diving off my grandmother's tower at 101st Street…lying under wet sheets when I got sunburned. I explain that my mom had also loved it here. My dad did, too, until he left. Which is why my mom doesn't come here very often anymore. It reminds her too much of him. She still brought me as a kid, every summer, or at least sent me to stay with my grandmother.

"This beach sustained me, it got me through the year, just thinking about it. I would even jump in the ocean one last time when our car was packed up, just to taste the salt in the tips of my braids the whole way home."

That starry night, to the hum of the air conditioner, Jamie and Eve make love for the first time. Outside, the rabbits quietly nibble their hay. White roses open their faces to the moon. A snowy owl glides low and slow over the house. And the Jersey Devil vanishes for good. Their dreams are briny and brackish.

☆

Sunday morning, over coffee in bed, I ask Jamie to tell me more about his work with troubled teens. He tells me that doctors refer teens to him for counseling, in hopes of avoiding the need to prescribe them antidepressants and other medications. Avoid, because the unintended side effects can be dangerous. Jamie's specialty is working with young men. He says that even "popular" kids are often struggling beneath their cheery veneers. High school is shitty for a lot of people. He helps them articulate their feelings and fears, encourages them to talk openly about self- medicating with pot and alcohol, while assuring them of complete confidentiality. He tells me that he only breaks this pact if the child is a danger to themselves or others or if they are being hurt by someone, often a parent. On a good day, he says, he manages to get through to a kid that while high school sometimes sucks, college really won't. Or, if they are not going to go to college, he helps them set goals towards employment and living on their own. On a bad day, he sometimes has to call a kid's physician about medication options, or worse, child welfare. In general he encourages kids to eat well, exercise a lot, watch less TV, get enough sleep, and "have a plan." Being a teenager is physically and emotionally hard. Jamie's job is to help kids "get over being teenagers." What an amazing job.

Saying goodbye to him Sunday is no fun, but he needs to help those kids, and they need him.

Pictures and Memories

The following weekend is rainy and unseasonably cold, soup weather. Saturday morning has us doing what couples do in bed on rainy Saturday mornings. Now I understand what all of the fuss is about. After, I guess because sex can sometimes also be baby making, my mind turns to little Bea.

"Where are you, Eve?"

"Sorry, far away. I was just thinking about back when I lost the baby. Sometimes when I try to remember the past, it's like I'm looking at pictures or watching a movie. I can't see that period of time from inside my own mind. Do you know what I mean? Are your memories like that? Are everyone's?"

"Hmm…I guess I never quite thought about it in specifically that way."

"I've tried to do it for various ages, and I *can* see my life happening and look through my own eyes as my third-grade self, seeing the kids at my new school when we moved halfway through the year. I can see and feel my memories all the way up until like, maybe twenty. Then it's all snapshots. I am remembering pictures of events instead of the real thing. If I didn't have photo albums…apparently I wouldn't have memories."

"Maybe you weren't really being true to yourself at twenty, or you were trying out new versions of you. Heading off to university is a big deal for pretty much everyone. It's huge but also super challenging, emotionally."

"Hmm…ya, but what if I'm still not seeing through true eyes? Will I only remember this summer as snapshots? I hate that."

"I think a person's life ends up looking more like chapters than a river of continuity, and a brain can only hold so many memories. It's natural that memories we've also seen pictures of can end up as the memory more of the photo, just the one moment, than the event."

"Photography is messing with us. Also, that makes me kind of sad."

"It's okay to be sad."

"Are you counseling me right here? Do I need to pay you like a hundred bucks right now?"

Jamie just stares at me and does that cute little downward head tilt. The damned dimple.

"Remind me to take more pictures this summer."

"You don't need to try to remember me Vee, I'm not going anywhere."

"Well…I still want to remember this summer. But can we really call photos memories? My brain hurts."

Later that day, Jamie and I are in his kitchen, making lunch and planning dinner. He didn't go swimming before lunch due to the weather. I am slicing onions and tomatoes when, out of the corner of my eye, I see him stretching his shoulders. He lengthens his body and places his hands behind his head, making that little sound people having a good stretch make. Now I am looking right at him. We had a stellar morning, but his tanned bare chest and bed head are doing things to me. How are his shoulders so muscled? He sits in a chair all week.

"Do all swimmers have bodies like yours?" He slowly turns towards me.

"No, Eve...I'm the only one," he says, staring straight into my eyes. I return his gaze with a smile. He continues toasting the bread.

"Pickles?" he asks.

"Every time," I reply.

"Can I give Ben some bacon? I always give a little piece to Daisy."

"Of course. I don't eat pigs, but, given the chance, Ben sure would. Tell me about your swimming. Have you always been a big swimmer?"

"Let me see...yup. I think I came out swimming. Living on the bay, it would be dangerous not to know how, so my parents taught me pretty early. It's too rough at the beach, past the waves, if the guards would even let you. I mean, you could wait 'til they leave at 5 p.m., but when I'm past the break, my mind goes automatically to sharks. The *Jaws* theme literally plays in my head."

"Same."

"So, I swim the bays."

"Multiple?"

"Sure, I can swim out of my bay and towards the inlet, just before you reach the point, and then back. You just have to check the tides, time it right. If I'm at all unsure, I just do laps in the bay. Clears my head."

"Is there a pool in your apartment building?"

"Ya, and it's empty at sunrise."

"What does Daisy do all day?"

"She comes with me. She's a great therapy dog. Some days, I leave her with my dad, if he's working from home, but usually she is with me. Right, Daisy May?"

"You love changing people's names, eh?"

"No, just Daisy and you. Vi."

"Vi as in eye."

"Vee as in *c'est la vie*. It changes, sometimes I feel very Vi-Vi about you, sometimes just Vi as in eye."

"Why? Wait…are we rhyming here? Should we become poets? I don't even like poetry. I think only toddlers and teenagers do." Again with the head tilt! "Back to swimming. I've told you about my grandparents having a bay house, right? My grandfather used to swim in the bay just like you do. My mom says he would actually swim out into the ocean and back. He was one of the first guards here. Later, he had to have one of his legs amputated, but he still swam laps every day."

"Eve, that's amazing. You should write a book about that."

"Maybe…someday. So, that explains your epic body."

"What explains yours?" he purrs, coming over to hug me from behind.

"You mean my scrawny little self?"

"No, I love your body. Do you still do any ballet?"

"No. When you aren't around stuffing my face with your amazing cooking, I survive on coffee and air. I wrecked my knees dancing, so I actually need to stay on the skinny side."

"You're perfect."

"Nobody's perfect."

"For me, you are perfect. Now, let's unhinge our jaws and eat these bodacious sandwiches."

"*Top Gun*?"

"*Top Gun* indeed."

We spend the rest of the afternoon watching *Top Gun*. I've seen it like ten times and love it every time. After the movie ends, I tell Jamie to take me to bed or lose me forever.

The Line

The following Saturday morning I wake up with Jamie spooning me. His hand is travelling slowly up and down my side. Hip, waist, ribs, repeat. I roll onto my back so his hand is on a new playing field. Ribs, stomach, ugh, I need to pee.

When I open the door to go back to bed, the light from the bathroom falls on his face, and I almost burn up on the spot. I close the door and the room returns to nearly dark. My blackout blinds do a pretty good job, but there's the glow of a hazy day spilling from around the edges. I climb back into bed. The hum of the air conditioner can't cover the crash of the waves. Jamie pulls me closer. I can feel and hear him smelling my hair.

"What do I smell like?"

"You, plus a little cinnamon."

"You usually smell like a mix of ocean and juniper."

"Mmm…my swimming and, I'm guessing, my deodorant."

His hand sliding down my body, stomach, hip, lower, silences us both. He rolls me onto my back and touches me for a few minutes, then his head disappears below the sheets. He gently starts tapping on me, like he's half patting me, half spanking me. I don't stop him. This is new. Then I feel his tongue lick me in a straight line from top to bottom, nice and slow. Then he returns to patting me, strategically, five or six times, but a little more firmly now, then the line.

I never even imagined a sex scene this steamy. Who would have thought anything could feel better than little circles. He always wants me to orgasm before we have sex, but this is special. I start fantasizing about a woman, a generic hottie, with teddy bear buns high on the sides of her head. *Pat, pat, pat, the line.* Jamie is holding her buns and she is giving him an impossibly good blowjob (impossible because no one actually likes to be slammed in the face). *Pat, pat, spank, the line, the line.* Then there's a second woman, and she starts licking the first one. Jamie is near coming in my fantasy, his head tilts back. *Pat, spank, spank, spank, the line, the line, the line.*

"I need you inside."

He switches to kneeling over me and slowly enters. I break into a million pieces. It rains a thousand daisies; they whip around and around the room. A whisper in my ear.

"Dorothy, come back to Kansas."

"Never."

Mirror Mirror

Next Saturday finds us enjoying a bay day. We make Caesars and Jamie grabs some bacon to set crab traps. A momma duck and nine babies are swimming in the middle of the bay. It's a hot, sunny day, so we both dive in. The tide is halfway out, so the dock is sitting low in the water. The barnacles and mussels are visible on the pilings. Ducks and crustaceans are about the only visible wildlife, and they are barely "wild" at that. Down deep is where the action is. Hopefully five or six bacon-loving crabs! I used to catch baby sharks fishing in the bay as a kid, but I try not to think about that right now.

Eve climbs up the dock's ladder with ease. I use my superpowers to erase her little yellow bikini. My superpower is definitely just my imagination, but my view is very super. Wet, her hair nearly reaches her bikini bottom. Her skin is light brown sugar. I've become so used to the smell of her sunscreen that literally anything coconut-scented gives me an erection. I think I've seen most of her jewelry by now. She rotates necklaces: tiny gold octopus, coral with a blue rope, and a silver conch shell. She always wears the same turquoise ring and never takes off her many silver bangles and one cuff. Her jewelry isn't showy, but she always wears some. Her makeup is subtle too. She hates to see women wearing makeup to the beach. I agree. In the safe, back at my apartment in the city, there's a pear cut diamond solitaire engagement ring. My mother wore it every day. I can already picture it on Eve's finger. Eve is self-reliant, she's been through some hard things and come out the other side braver than before. She doesn't need protecting maybe, but I feel protective towards her.

"Come here."

"You want me to sit on your lap?" she says.

"Yes, you look cold."

After baking in the sun for an hour, we rinse off in the outside shower and head upstairs to get dressed. But Jamie has other plans for me. I can see it in his eyes as soon as we enter his bedroom. The room is eggshell white with deep blue accents. The king-size bed is covered in a royal blue blanket. There are wooden seagulls on one of the walls. The doors to the balcony are open, but the sheer curtains are drawn, a light breeze causing them to billow. He takes his white towel off, then walks towards me. He gently takes my towel, kisses me tenderly, then takes my hand and leads me to his mirrored closet doors. He kisses me again, then kneels down. Watching us is nearly as good as being us. In the end, the wall stands in for the bed.

Later that afternoon, Jamie asks me if I want to go on a bike ride. In his garage, there are multiple upright handled bikes with baskets. We hop on and I follow him. First we ride the three blocks to the beach. Then, passing the bird sanctuary, we head to the point. We lock our bikes to the fence and walk the rest of the way. In addition to a couple of white stones, we find a perfect sand dollar, bleached by the sun, a charcoal colored scallop shell, and what Jamie still calls a unicorn horn shell. Shells are a hobby of mine. When you grow up thinking about one particular beach all year long, a shell obsession can be forgiven. Whenever I have visited other beaches, I have been disappointed. No rainbow clams under your feet at the water's edge. No tall white wooden lifeguard chairs. No row boats with the town's name in red on the side. Where are the hospital green water towers? Why isn't the sand more like powder and less like, well…sand? Don't get me wrong, I worship every beach I see. In Vancouver, I drove into the pull-out on the road coming back from UBC to see the ocean one hundred percent of the times I was on that stretch of road. But the first time I saw logs on the beaches there, my eyebrows tried to leave my face. I got used to it eventually. But it's just not New Jersey.

That night, Jamie introduces a new game called rights of nonrefusal. Basically, anytime, day or night, if one of us puts the moves on the other, it's game on. I'm not sure how this will work. At 3 a.m. Jamie wakes me up to show me exactly how this works, and now I understand. It reminds you to make the other person feel something so special: that they are deeply *wanted*.

Skinny Dip

The following Saturday I wake up to brilliant sunshine seeping out from the edges of my blinds. Jamie is next to me, having decided not to go for his usual sunrise walk. I wake him with a kiss. I feed the bunnies, chickens, and Brownie while Jamie makes blueberry pancakes. By the time the noon horn sounds, we are in our spot at the beach. The sun is white hot today, and there's barely a breeze. You know what that means. Horseflies. I always keep a flyswatter in my beach bag. Today there's also a can of Diet Coke and a bag of Snyder's Hard Pretzels.

I am reading *A Fine Balance* by Rohinton Mistry on Eve's advice. It's a hard read; the story is heart wrenching, but the writing is spellbinding. And so is Eve today. She is wearing a black strapless bathing suit, high cut on the sides, making her beautiful legs look miles long, even though she is barely 5'4". She is wearing her huge, black movie-star sunglasses. She is my sexy little bug. Okay eyes, back to reading before I use my rights of nonrefusal card and get us arrested.

I am reading *The Fall* by Albert Camus today. It's only 147 pages, and I am on page 97, so I should be able to finish it this afternoon. I read it in high school and I just didn't get it, not really. I think you need to have lived a little before you can see the layers in things. Jamie said to think of it as *Crime and Punishment* meets Dante's *Inferno*, but set in Amsterdam. Later today I am making veggie pâté and apricot-turmeric jam to bring to the market tomorrow. I almost wish I didn't have to work on weekends when Jamie is here. Actually, I wish he didn't have to be gone during the week. I know that I'm starting to care too much, but honestly, I don't feel the way I used to feel about it, about him, about love. I look over at him. His skin is deeply tanned and it suits him. He's wearing cranberry red board shorts courtesy of Billabong. The hair on his chest is golden; it narrows to a trail that disappears into his shorts. The hair on his head has blonde tips now from so much time in the water and sun. He rolls back onto his stomach to keep reading and catches me staring at him.

Lowering his sunglasses, he says "Don't look at me like that, Vi."

"You can't even see my eyes!"

"The lust is rolling off you in waves, woman."

"Dammit."

"Let me see your eyes."

I remove my sunglasses. "What do you see?"

"I see you. I see turtle green with a deep green rim. There's a brownish fleck in the green on your left eye. I can see forever."

"Wow…that was deep."

"I'm deep."

"Actually, yes, you are. I love that about you."

"How about my eyes?"

"Well, they look like the water. You have ocean eyes. Lucky. Wanna trade?"

"No. Wanna go for a walk? You can show off your strangely thorough knowledge of shell names. What did you tell me rainbow clams are really called?"

"Coquina."

"Mmm…you're a cockina."

"That didn't even make sense."

"Yes, it did."

We walk past lifeguard chair after lifeguard chair. This island is over five miles long, so we couldn't walk it all. But I would love to punk physics and never let this day end. For eternity I want to be walking this exact beach with her. Maybe people fall in love at first sight all of the time, but if it turns out not to be the one, they forget it ever happened. But because I have turned out to be right about her, the memory is still fresh for me. Her, on her faded blue blanket. Her cream-colored shawl wrapped around her. Her beautiful face looking out to sea. Her expression, a mix of sadness and awe, like it was her first sunrise. I will never forget that morning.

She is telling me about the funny little rubbery jellyfish in her hand, how they can't sting you and have four gonads or something crazy like that. Just then, I spot a big shell, the kind your aunt uses as an ashtray.

"Okay, so what amazing name does this one have?"

"Clam."

"Seriously?"

"Atlantic surf clam, bivalve, mollusk…but, ya, *clam.*"

"Surfing clams are the coolest."

"No, quahogs are the best because they are better raw than oysters and make the greatest soup of all time. Did you know that littlenecks, topnecks, and cherrystones are just quahogs in different sizes?"

"I guess I never really thought about it. Do you like razor clams too?"

"Yup."

"So you eat all seafoods, but no farm animals."

"If I couldn't kill it myself, I'm not eating it."

"I can see your point. What's your favorite fish?"

"Salmon. Vancouver did that right."

"What about local? Maybe you want to go fishing with me and my friend Johnny some time?"

"I would love that. And, I like flounder. My mom says my dad used to make it for me when I was little. Dredged in flour and orange salt, served with lemon and cocktail sauce. I'd eat cardboard if it had a side of cocktail sauce."

"Amen," I say as we continue scanning the sand for treasure. "What about the shells that look like snail shells but a little bigger and prettier?"

"Shark eye or moonsnail. Wanna know why clam shells often have that perfect little hole in them, so every ten year old girl can make a necklace?"

"Is that why?"

"Jamie."

"Sorry."

"Okay. So, moonsnails crawl onto them, release acid that makes the hole, then eat the clam."

"That's terrifying. That's worse than *Jaws*."

"Nothing is worse than *Jaws*, Jamie."

We arrive back at the blanket and decide to play a game. We are going to psych ourselves out talking about sharks, then try to swim just past the break while making the *Jaws* sound, *da-na, da-na, da-na*. Jamie tells me the story of how it all started. There was a polio epidemic in 1916 (1918 wasn't much better—hello, Spanish flu), and in July of that year, it was extremely hot, so a lot of people flocked to the beaches. Like you do. In the space of just ten days, four people were attacked and killed, and one more was attacked and survived. All on the Jersey Shore. The attacks were the inspiration for the novel *Jaws*, which was later made into a movie.

"I already can't go swimming now!"

"Okay, baby, maybe later."

Definitely later as it turns out. That night Jamie surprises me with a rights of nonrefusal proposition. "Let's do it on the beach." I'm game. I just finished a martini that James Bond would *actually* die for, and that man is hard to kill. So, yeah, sandy sex seems like a great idea. We step outside, look up at the stars, link hands, and begin walking. The buzzing sound is nothing compared to the electricity buzzing in my body. When we arrive at the beach, we are greeted by a truly enormous full moon on the horizon.

"Did you plan this in advance?" I ask Jamie.

"I mean, I want to take credit, but I did not. The universe manufactured it because the moon loves love."

After, because Jamie screwed my brains out and I can't even remember that sharks are a thing, we go skinny dipping. We stay pretty shallow because even gentle surf is still ocean and demands to be respected. As we walk home, Jamie whispers in my ear, "You do know that sharks are more likely to come into the shallows at night."

"Jesus."

Sunday morning, while lying in bed, Jamie asks me what being pregnant was like. It's a question none of my friends had asked. Even my own mother never spoke of my pregnancy, as if it was somehow shameful to bring up. Mostly people had said "it's God's will," or "nature's way," or worse, "it happens all the time." I felt like I was just supposed to forget it, and for sure I was never supposed to bring it up. He then asks me what it actually *felt* like. Something blossoms inside of me as I begin to tell him.

"It was like magic. The day I found out, my period was only one day late. I took one test, then to be sure, another one. And I kid you not, later that day, I peed on a third stick.

"I was so excited, I walked around like I had a baby bunny in my pocket that I needed to show every person I met. I had heard people say that you're not supposed to tell people until you're three months along, but I couldn't wait. Also, if you don't tell your people that you're pregnant, how are they supposed to help you through a miscarriage? Little did I know, our culture, our society, doesn't have words for how to let or help a woman grieve that loss.

"I didn't know I only had five months to love that baby, but I had been wanting a baby since I was about twelve, so I was very excited. Very. The nausea tamped down some of my enthusiasm in the first three months, usually just in the morning. In the good moments, I was a temple. I could *make* a person, much better than a person…a baby.

"I read books on pregnancy, ate healthier, planned my delivery, and rubbed my tiny tummy. My fourth month, I was feeling better than new, and I actually felt myself glowing. I imagined what delivery would be like. I was terrified, actually. More importantly, I pictured holding the baby for the first time. I imagined the toddler version of him or her walking next to me, holding my hand.

"I bought a few onesies and embroidered flowers on them, and socks so small they make your heart ache. I bought a baby rattle and a little stuffed bunny. And some books. Children's books are so underrated."

"I love children's books," Jamie says. "I am thirty years old and I still want to read *Goodnight Gorilla*, even if the only words in it are 'goodnight' and 'gorilla.'"

"I still have everything in a box in the attic. The first book I bought was a flip the flap version of *Peter Rabbit*."

"Good choice, and can we please get flip the flap books for grown-ups?"

"Right?"

I tell him about my last month of having a baby living inside of me. I never took it for granted, thank God. I thought about her (I'd started to think it was a girl but wanted a boy just as much) day and night. I talked to her, sang to her, held her by holding my own growing tummy, like a magic orb. Every kick was a tiny miracle. You never know how much you could miss something until it's gone.

"Those memories haunted me for a long time."

"And now…?"

"Now I cherish them. I disagree that you're supposed to try to forget. I don't obsess about it. It happened. It's over. But it was a very special time. I have no desire to pretend she never was. They let me see her. My body ached for her to be back inside, safe. I felt hollow…. Well, there you have it."

"Last question: had you named her while you were pregnant?"

"I've only said her name out loud once. After it was over, nobody asked me her name, and Scott said you don't have funerals for miscarriages."

"Oh, shit."

"I had a few names in mind, for both boys and girls. When I saw her, I knew she was a Beatrice. Little Bea, that's how I think of her."

I can't talk about her (I never have, not using her name) or think about her without tears filling my eyes. When one escapes, Jamie reaches up and slowly wipes it away with his warm thumb.

"When they took her away, and Scott had gone— he handled all of the details—I was alone. I looked down at my empty hands and said her little name, just so I could ever have said it. I never even got to hold her."

"Was there a why?"

"No."

"That's hard. Not that it would have fixed anything, but knowing why something happened often helps. Otherwise you're just left with how unfair life can be."

"Yeah. I comfort myself in knowing that she never knew what she missed. If there are angels, they are all the lost souls of tiny babies."

"That's beautiful."

"Tragic and beautiful."

"They often go together. Right?"

"Right."

Barrier Islands

Over the next few weekends, Jamie and I explored the Jersey coast. Because I only got to come to the shore once a year, and only for a couple of weeks, I had really only ever seen our town and maybe two others, Wildwood and Cape May. Everyone visits the boardwalk in Wildwood at least once. Cape May is also worth the trip if you like charming Victorian era houses, and, really, who doesn't?

We started up north and made our way south, visiting a few places a day and trying to stick to the bridges that link the islands. We went to busy Seaside Heights and quieter Long Beach (eighteen miles to be exact). We ate at Busch's in Sea Isle City. It has been there since 1812. I hope it never closes.

We had soft shell crabs, cooked to perfection, divine steamed clams with melted butter, and those classic little house salads in wooden bowls. We did not have the snapper soup, as our parents definitely would have.

Jamie shared his love of fish, sharks, rays, and whales with me. Unsettlingly, I learned that hammerhead sharks have been spotted in as little as three feet of water, our water, here. We have three types of sea turtles: loggerhead, leatherback, and the green turtle. He explained why conservation efforts towards horseshoe crabs are so important, not just to save these living dinosaurs, but as part of a wider link in the ecosystem. Snowbirds, migratory shore birds, stop off on their way north to rest and eat horseshoe crab eggs. I learned these tidbits and many more at Busch's. Watching Jamie talk so animatedly about something he was so passionate about made me fall a little bit more in love with him.

We developed rituals during this time. He continued his sunrise walks but always returned to bed with a gift from the sea. We had coffee in bed, then he went swimming in the bay while I took care of my garden and animals. On Sunday mornings, he would make a donut run to Britton's, the best bakery in all of Jersey. Apple fritter for me, raised glazed for him.

On the beach in Cedar Bonnet (one of the tiniest islands), Jamie told me something about seahorses that changed my life forever. Seahorses, ours are called lined seahorses, are actually fish; this I knew. But the way he explained their bonds was positively romantic. Seahorses mate for life, but it gets better: each morning, as the sun illuminates their world, they perform a ritual dance to strengthen their bond. They entwine their tails, embracing, and make clicking sounds while changing color. He suggested we steal their idea. I could expect Jamie to take my hand and twirl me into an embrace every morning that we were together for the foreseeable future.

During these exploratory weekends, Jamie didn't bring up our relationship at all. I now understood that he was giving me time. Whatever his plan was, it worked. We loved a lot of the same things and couldn't get enough of each other. I came to really know him on those drives. And we listened to a lot of good music, even some bands that didn't start with "the," though I must say, Sting sang *Every Breath You Take* to us on many a road. We frequently stopped at the Wawa for coffee as we arrived back in town and headed to the beach to watch it empty of sun worshippers. There's something in the way lifeguards blow their whistles and everyone leaves the water that suits my soul. Hazelnut Wawa coffee at 5 p.m. came to be a part of that.

I learned that Jamie only liked one flavor of ice cream: chocolate. He marveled at the chameleon wizardry of my flavor choices, rum raisin one week, mint chocolate chip the next. But we both agreed on this: Springer's has the best ice cream. They have our loyalty for life. We also decided that although a lot of the beaches we visited were beautiful, ours is really the only one that feels just right.

On the way to go fishing with Jamie's friend John in Cape May, we stopped in at Star Diner for brunch (I'll be back) and made a side trip to Diamond Beach. My parents met there, so I really wanted to see it. It was covered in sunbathers and beach chairs, but I'm still glad I got to see it. I could almost feel them falling in love. He swept her off her feet, she never really did come down.

The only sea life we saw were dolphins, or porpoises? Only Jamie knew the difference. The good news was that we caught enough fish for an early dinner. Jamie and John cooked it right on the boat. I could get used to this life. We didn't see any great white sharks…but I knew they were out there. We made it back in time to get Wawa coffee and start a new tradition, walking Brownie on our "no dogs allowed before 5 p.m." beach. While we were walking, Jamie, who knew that I loved octopuses, told me that they have three hearts and that one of their arms acts as a penis. I still love them anyway. If I had three hearts, they would all beat for Jamie.

Sea Fireflies

One evening, Jamie brought me to Manasquan Beach. It was a crisp evening, and we were huddled beneath a large blanket from his car, waiting. On the drive there, Jamie had told me that sometimes you can see bioluminescence in the water here. "Umihotaru" he called it, which translates to *sea fireflies.* He went on to describe how the Japanese, during WWII, harvested these tiny crustaceans, dried them, then powdered them. Then, when needed, added water and the mix produced enough glow to read a map by. I was amazed but was about to be amazed even further. Imagining bioluminescent waves and really seeing them are two very different things.

As the sun gave its final farewell, the water began to glow, supernatural, like the sun impregnating the sea. We waited. Jamie explained that the enzyme involved in bioluminescence is called luciferase. I replied that a better name might be *angelase,* the magic involved in glowing. As the sky faded to black, the moon glowed brighter. And then it began. I can only describe it as an aurora borealis of the sea, ethereal, like the dawn of a new day.

The End

Jamie and I talk during the week, every night in fact, and we agree: no more games. Well, rights of nonrefusal might stick around. I ask him if that means I can't ask him to dress up like a fireman for me. He says, "Anytime, babe." We are trying to move forward with open minds and hearts.

Friday night, I wait up late for Jamie. He had to work late and won't get in until nearly midnight. I doze off and am awoken with a kiss on my forehead.

"I'm here, go back to sleep."

"I need to hug you and stuff."

"We can 'and stuff' in the morning, Vi. Sleep. I'll be right in."

I find him half an hour later on the porch patting Ben, Daisy at his feet, a nearly empty glass of Scotch in his hand.

"Jamie?"

"Sorry, Evie, just processing some stuff. I'll be in soon, promise."

I love that he can focus on his feelings, then move forward. I want him to teach me how.

I am still awake when he comes to bed.

"Rough day at work, eh?"

"Eve...I wasn't thinking about work. I was thinking about you."

My heart speeds up. This is the part where he breaks my heart, where he says "let's talk in the morning," but I press him on it, and he says "it's over" or, worse, that he found somebody else.

"Evie? You're awful quiet for someone I just told I stayed up late thinking about."

"If it's over, I'd rather you just tell me now. I won't be able to sleep wondering."

"Eve...I was thinking that I am in love with you and wondering if it was safe to tell you."

"You love me?"

"Yes, I do. I have loved you from the first time I laid eyes on you. I think the dogs knew before I did, but I knew pretty quick."

"Jamie, I love you too. What do we do now?"

"We take it slow. But know this, Eve, I love you very much and I intend to spend the rest of my life proving it to you."

And he did.

Epilogue

This is how we must love it, faithful and
fleeting. I wed the sea.
        —Albert Camus, *The Sea Close By*

When I look back on our life together, I know that
Jamie was a gift to me. He gave me the time I needed
to fulfill my dreams and build what is still my life
today, what sustains me in every sense of the word.
He believed in our love until I did.

If you want Jamie and me to live on forever like
all great romances, to live happily ever after, to never
really end—if that's what you need—then close this
book right now. I love to think that somewhere out
there our love lives on, uninterrupted.

You're still here, so here it is. Jamie did spend
the rest of his life proving it to me. He loved me full

stop. In time, like a wave crashing in slow motion, I came to love him fully too. We married two years after the day we met, on the anniversary of the exact date, at sunrise. Ben and Daisy by our sides. I never did really become a sunrise girl; I left that to Jamie and the dogs, and sometimes his mom, I suspect. He never skipped our seahorse morning bonding ritual, twirling me around the kitchen Saturday after Saturday after Saturday. He moved to working mainly from home, only going into the city three days a week. Home became my little yellow house, with its outdoor shower, two dogs, ten rabbits, fourteen chickens, and one very small pony. We rented out the bay house for most of the summer but used it for ourselves the last week of July and the first week of August. We never had children, though we tried. But mostly, we were happy. Over the years, we filled a huge bowl with white stones of the flat and round variety. I find them still, and a little bit, they are him.

Ten years after we met, Jamie was hit by a drunk driver and killed instantly. Staring out to sea is more about blank spaces and air, less about water, like trying to see through time. Sometimes I dream about him; a tsunami washes him back to me. He looks so real, so alive, that I wake up already crying.

This book stands as a testament to our love, as beautiful as the sea. My kind and gentle, my quiet, husband. I spread his ashes at N 39°3′14″ W 74°45′34″, just beyond the waves.

Those who love and are separated can live in grief, but this is not despair: they know that love exists.
—Albert Camus, *The Sea Close By*

Afterword

Twilight is a time out of time. That time in between asleep and awake is when I can most clearly remember him. What it felt like to be in his arms. How warm his body was. The smell of him. How the sunlight filled the room…the last time.

It has taken me years to write this. Thank God I remember it. If you ever lose someone, climb up off the floor long enough to write down as many of your "for the last times" as you can remember. You need to get those cherished, sharp, glaring memories out of you and onto paper, so they don't completely tear you apart.

I eventually learned to put all of our "for the last times" into a kind of snow globe of the mind and set it aside. I know it's what he would have wanted. He never wanted to see me sad, so he certainly wouldn't have wanted to see me ruined.

Writing this has helped me see our story through my own eyes…and sometimes his. I never want my memories of him to become just photographs.

When I feel the need, I take out the snow globe and give it a little shake. Sometimes—like when I wrote this book—it gives me not just all of the "for the last times," but also all of the "for the first times."

About the Author

Lauren Flanagan has three sisters and three brothers. She attended McGill University and is married to a man she met her first week there. Together, they have three children: Aislinn, Keegan, and Brenna. They also have two dogs. She lives and writes in Vancouver, Canada, but her heart belongs to the unnamed town in *I Wed the Sea,* her debut novel.

Follow Lauren on her bookish Instagram page @laurengflanagan_reads.

Hi!

I hope you
enjoyed I Wed
the Sea.

:)

Lauren Flanagan

CPSIA information can be obtained
at www.ICGtesting.com
Printed in the USA
BVHW081800030321
601249BV00002B/7

9 781771 804769